ULTIMATE STICKER COLLECTION

How to use this book

Read the captions, then find
the sticker that best fits the space.
(Hint: check the sticker labels for clues!)

There are lots of fantastic
extra stickers, too!

DK | Penguin Random House

Written by Julia March, Lauren Nesworthy, Susan Reuben, and Lisa Stock
Edited by Lisa Stock and Lauren Nesworthy
Designed by Clive Savage, Lynne Moulding, and Chris Gould
Jacket designed by Lynne Moulding

First American Edition, 2019
Published in the United States by DK Publishing
1450 Broadway, Suite 801, New York, NY 10018

First published as two separate titles. Contains content previously published in
Frozen Ultimate Sticker Collection (2015) and Frozen 2: Magical Sticker Book (2019).

Page design copyright © 2019 Dorling Kindersley Limited
DK, a Division of Penguin Random House LLC
21 22 23 10 9 8
008–316979–Oct/2019

A catalog record for this book is available from the Library of Congress.
ISBN 978-1-4654-9209-8

DK books are available at special discounts when purchased in bulk for sales
promotions, premiums, fund-raising, or educational use.
For details, contact: DK Publishing Special Markets,
1450 Broadway, Suite 801, New York, NY 10018. SpecialSales@dk.com

Printed and bound in China

A WORLD OF IDEAS:
SEE ALL THERE IS TO KNOW
www.dk.com

Welcome to Arendelle

The kingdom of Arendelle is beautiful and harmonious. The people there live very happily and peacefully, but little do they know, behind the castle walls lies an icy secret that could change all of their lives forever.

© Disney

Close sisters

Arendelle is home to two princesses named Elsa and Anna. The sisters are very different, but when they were young they were the best of friends.

© Disney

King and Queen

Elsa and Anna's parents are the King and Queen of Arendelle. They are fair rulers, and are loved by their people. They will do anything to keep their daughters safe.

© Disney

Castle

The royal family lives in a grand castle. Its ancient bridges, soaring turrets, and pointed green spires make it the most spectacular building in Arendelle.

Lush land

Arendelle is full of natural beauty. The kingdom has many lush, green gardens and is surrounded by great forests, where animals are free to roam.

© Disney

Duke

The Duke of Weselton is not to be trusted. The scheming Duke is determined to get his greedy hands on Arendelle's riches.

© Disney

© Disney

Icy mountains

Beyond the kingdom, there are snow-capped mountains that stretch as far as the eye can see. Hardworking men climb them and cut the ice from the high mountain lakes to sell.

Fjord

The fastest way to get in or out of Arendelle is by crossing the sparkling fjord on a ship. The fjord is also used to transport valuable goods to trade.

Elsa

Princess Elsa was born with incredible icy powers. She is gentle and caring, so she is afraid of hurting people with her magic. Elsa wears gloves to help her conceal her powers and spends her days shut away from the world.

Living in fear

After Elsa accidentally hurts Anna with her powers, she decides to stay away from her younger sister, and even avoids her parents. She is desperate not to hurt anyone else.

© Disney

Sisters in the snow

Elsa used to love using her magic to have fun with her sister, Anna. Playtime for the princesses involved ice-skating in the Great Hall and building snowmen.

© Disney

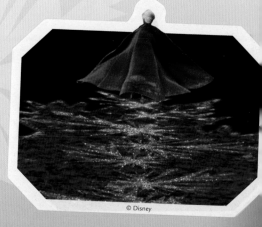

© Disney

The new queen

When Elsa turns 21, she is crowned Queen of Arendelle. The coronation makes her very nervous—will she be able to hide her magic from all those people?

© Disney

Runaway

When Elsa's secret is revealed in front of the entire kingdom, she decides to flee from Arendelle. As she runs across the fjord, the water turns to ice under her feet.

Stay away

Elsa hides away on the North Mountain, where she creates a beautiful ice palace. She may be alone, but at least she is finally free to unleash her powers and be herself.

© Disney

No way out

Some of the people in Arendelle believe that Elsa is dangerous. She is captured, locked in the dungeons, and forced to wear iron gloves to stop her magic.

© Disney

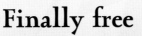

© Disney

Finally free

When Elsa lets go of her fears, she learns to control her powers. She can finally share her magic safely with the people of Arendelle—and her sister!

Anna

Princess Anna is playful and fearless—if a little clumsy! The trolls erased all her memories of Elsa's powers after that early icy accident, and now she can't understand why her sister ignores her.

Knock, knock

After Anna's accident, Elsa shuts herself away. Anna keeps knocking on Elsa's door, hoping that one day it will finally open. She wishes that her sister would play with her again.

© Disney

Lonely lif

Without Elsa, life in the cas is pretty lonely for Ann She spends her days trying find ways to pass the tim Balancing on a bicyc is a lot of fu

© Disney

New beginning?

As Elsa is crowned Queen of Arendelle, Anna stands by her sister's side. She hopes that this celebration will help them become close again.

A brave journey

Anna may be shocked by Elsa's powers, but now she understands why Elsa stayed away. Despite the freezing snow, Anna is determined to find her sister and bring her home.

New friends

Anna's quest to find Elsa is a dangerous one. Thankfully, she meets an ice harvester named Kristoff, his reindeer Sven, and a warm-hearted snowman named Olaf. They help her along the way.

Struck!

When Elsa strikes Anna with an icy blast of magic, the princess's heart begins to freeze. Unless she is saved by an act of true love, she will turn to ice forever!

Anna's plea

Elsa insists that she can't stop the eternal winter in Arendelle. Anna tries to convince her that if they work together, they can find a way to fix things.

Coronation Day

When Princess Elsa turns 21, the time comes for her to be crowned Queen of Arendelle. The castle gates will finally be opened and people will be allowed inside—but only for one day. This will truly be a celebration to remember!

Important day

No one is more excited for the coronation than Anna! She cannot wait for the empty castle to finally be filled with new people.

Full of hope

Anna imagines meeting a charming stranger at the coronation ball. The celebrations will last for just one day, so this may be her only chance to meet someone special!

Opening gates

For such a special occasion, the castle gates are opened for the first time in years! The people of Arendelle are excited for Elsa to become queen.

Keep control

Elsa is afraid that her nerves will cause her to reveal her magic. She tries to remember what her father taught her—conceal it, don't feel it, don't let it show!

Honored guests

Dignitaries from far and wide watch Elsa being crowned queen. But a handsome prince from the Southern Isles only has eyes for Princess Anna.

Grand ceremony

The ceremony takes place in Arendelle's magnificent chapel. Despite Elsa's fears, she does her best to appear calm and poised—just as a queen should be.

Time to dance

After the ceremony, the guests enjoy a grand ball. After years of silence, the castle ballroom is filled with music and dancing, as well as delicious food!

The truth comes out

Elsa tries to enjoy the ball, but an argument with Anna causes her to lose her cool. When Anna pulls off one of Elsa's gloves, Elsa accidentally reveals her magic!

Prince Hans

Prince Hans of the Southern Isles is smart, sophisticated, and incredibly handsome. Hans may seem like a charming gentleman, but he is nothing of the sort. He longs to have a kingdom of his own, and will stop at nothing to get it.

© Disney

Perfect prince

When Hans meets Anna on Coronation Day, he wastes no time sweeping her off her feet. He knows that the easiest way for him to become a king is to marry a princess.

© Disney

Icy battle

Hans is not afraid to face Elsa's icy powers. If he captures the queen, his scheming to become king might just work.

© Disney

Taking charge

While Anna searches for Elsa, Hans is left in charge of Arendelle. By acting like a strong, trustworthy leader, he wins the hearts of the people.

Power play

After Elsa is captured, Hans tries to gain her trust by pretending that he wants to help her. He tells Elsa to stop the winter, but she doesn't know how to!

© Disney

Cold as ice

Anna was sure that Hans would save her by giving her true love's kiss. But instead, he finally reveals his true colors!

© Disney

Becoming king

Hans tells many lies to get his way. He pretends that he and Anna were married, and that she has died. The dignitaries decide that this now makes Hans the king—just as he planned!

© Disney

Final fight

Hans knows that he cannot truly become king until he gets rid of Elsa once and for all. He chases her through the icy storm and almost defeats her. Fortunately, Anna arrives just in time to stop him!

© Disney

Exposed

When the winter is lifted from Arendelle, everyone sees Hans for the power-hungry prince he truly is. His 12 older brothers will not be happy with him!

A royal engagement

Anna is excited to meet new people at Elsa's coronation—but nothing can prepare her for meeting Prince Hans. As the day goes on, the two grow closer, until Anna is certain that Hans must be her true love. She is overjoyed to have finally found someone who understands her.

© Disney

Charmed

Anna and Hans first bump into each other by the fjord. When Hans realizes that Anna is a princess, he bows gallantly. Anna can't help falling for such a charming prince.

© Disney

Shall we dance?

Handsome Hans asks Anna to dance with him at the ball and she does not hesitate to accept. The two share an elegant waltz—Hans is the perfect partner!

Opening up

Hans tells Anna about his 12 older brothers, and she tells him about Elsa. Hans swears that he would never shut Anna out the way that Elsa did.

© Disney

Perfect pair

Hans and Anna both shout "jinx!" when they say the same thing at the same time. They are so similar—they must be made for each other.

True love

Before the night is over, Hans asks Anna to marry him—and she says yes! She may have only known him for one day, but why wait when you've found true love?

Shock announcement

The happy couple rushes to tell Elsa about their engagement. However, their news leads to a terrible argument between the sisters, and Elsa's icy powers are revealed.

Kristoff

Kristoff is an ice harvester who likes to do his own thing and doesn't care what people think of him. He is very strong and knows how to survive in the rugged mountains around Arendelle. Kristoff may act tough, but deep down, he has a warm and gentle heart.

Mountain boy

When Kristoff was a boy he loved to collect ice with his beloved reindeer Sven. He never gave up, even though the ice blocks were slippery and very heavy.

First impressions

The first time Anna meets Kristoff, he is covered in snow and ice from head to toe. He is rude and unfriendly and she is not impressed by him at all!

Reindeer duet

Kristoff sings and plays his lute for Sven before they go to sleep. Sometimes, he pretends that Sven is singing along with him!

Helpful plan

Kristoff sees that Anna's hair is turning white because Elsa has frozen her heart. He is sure that his friends, the "love experts," will be able to help her.

Ultimate ice sculpture

Kristoff is completely in awe when he sees Elsa's ice palace. Ice is his life and he has never seen it made into something so beautiful before.

Troll friends

Kristoff's friends are a family of trolls who adopted him when he was a little boy. They are very eager for Kristoff to get married. Maybe a little too eager!

Sled upgrade

Anna gives Kristoff a new sled to make up for the one he lost when he was helping her. It is the latest model and he is thrilled with it!

Olaf

Olaf is a snowman who was brought to life by Elsa. He is always cheerful, and although he does not understand much about the world, he knows a great deal about love and friendship. His greatest wish is to experience summer!

Snowy playmate

Young Elsa and Anna build a snowman together in the castle's Great Hall. Elsa calls him Olaf. The princesses giggle as they glide around on the icy floor with Olaf between them.

Warm introductions

At first, Anna and Kristoff are alarmed to meet a walking, talking snowman. But happy and curious Olaf soon wins them over—he loves making new friends!

Heads up

Olaf's nose, arms, and even his head, often come off during his adventures. It never does him any harm, but he prefers to be all in one piece!

© Disney

In summer

Olaf has always dreamed of enjoying a nice, hot summer's day. He has no idea that snowmen melt in the heat!

© Disney

Keeping cool

As soon as summer comes back to Arendelle, poor Olaf begins to melt ... until Elsa gives him his own personal snow flurry.

© Disney

Sven

Sven is Kristoff's loyal companion and accompanies him on all his adventures. He is playful and brave, and is always willing to help people—especially if they offer him delicious carrots in return!

Warm-hearted reindeer

Sven always tries to make Kristoff do the right thing. He may not talk like a human, but he can be very persuasive.

Furry friend

Kristoff and Sven have always been a great team. Even when they were little, they collected ice together, just like the grown-ups.

Speedy Sven

Sven has a great sense of adventure, and loves galloping through the snow. He and Kristoff like to go fast!

Slipping

Sven's hooves are made for walking in the snow, not climbing icy staircases. With nothing to grip he finds it hard not to slide straight back down!

Tasty treats

Sven's favorite snack is a crunchy carrot. As long as he has a regular supply, he is happy.

Elsa's powers

Elsa has always been afraid of hurting people with her magic. But once her icy secret is out she is free to find out what her powers can really do! She discovers that she can make amazing things out of ice and even create living snowmen.

Eternal winter

Elsa does not realize that she has set off an eternal winter in Arendelle. Even though it is summer-time, everything is covered in thick snow and the fjord is frozen solid.

Beautiful patterns

Elsa forms the ice and snow into stunningly beautiful patterns in the air. She finally feels powerful and free.

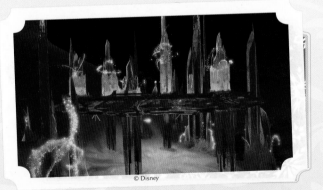

Ice palace

Elsa uses her powers to create a magnificent ice palace. It shines brightly across the mountains and seems to change color according to Elsa's mood.

New look

Elsa creates a dazzling gown for herself to match her new-found freedom. It sparkles with thousands of shimmering snowflakes.

Defense

The Duke of Weselton's two thugs try to attack Elsa, but they do not realize how strong her powers are. She stops them in their tracks with dangerous blasts of magic.

© Disney

Marshmallow

Elsa creates Marshmallow, a huge snow creature, to escort Anna, Kristoff, and Olaf off the mountain. Spikes pop out of his body when he gets angry—he will do anything to protect Elsa!

© Disney

© Disney

Fun on the ice

Just because summer has returned to Arendelle doesn't mean there can be no more ice. Queen Elsa creates a magical ice rink in the castle courtyard for her people to enjoy.

The trolls

The trolls are mysterious creatures who live in the mountains around Arendelle. They have gained a lot of wisdom over hundreds of years, so they are great at giving advice. Kristoff considers the trolls his closest friends, but he still hates it when they try to matchmake!

Meet the trolls

The trolls are made of stone and can disguise themselves as mossy boulders. However, when they come to life, they can be quite loud!

Grand Pabbie

Grand Pabbie is the leader of the trolls. He is very old and knows a great deal about magic. He always uses this knowledge to help those in need.

Worried royals

When Elsa accidentally hurts young Anna with her powers, the king immediately takes Anna to the trolls. He knows that they are the only ones who can help her.

Magic expert

Powerful Grand Pabbie heals Anna after her icy accident. He changes her memories so that she forgets about Elsa's magic. He then tells Elsa that she must learn to control her powers.

Happy family

The trolls are very kind creatures. When motherly troll Bulda meets young Kristoff and Sven, she cannot resist adopting them. The trolls raise them as part of the family.

Meeting Anna

When Kristoff introduces Anna to the trolls, they are very excited to meet her. They are overjoyed that he has found such a nice girl to love!

Epic journey

At first, Kristoff and Anna do not get along ... at all! Kristoff thinks that Anna is bossy and Anna thinks that Kristoff is grouchy. But as they experience danger and fun together on their journey to find Elsa, they start to appreciate each other.

Frosty beginnings

Kristoff did not want anything to do with Anna. But when Anna tells him that she knows how to stop the winter, he agrees to help her.

© Disney

Disagreements

Kristoff can't believe that Anna has agreed to marry a man she has just met. Anna insists that Hans is her true love, but Kristoff isn't so sure.

© Disney

A daring escape

When Marshmallow chases Anna and Kristoff, they must work together in order to escape. The pair start learning how to trust each other.

© Disney

Troll wedding

The trolls decide that Anna is the perfect girl for their Kristoff. Before they know it, the pair almost becomes a "trollfully" wedded husband and wife!

© Disney

To the rescue

When Kristoff sees a terrifying storm swirling above Arendelle, he realizes that Anna is in danger. He and Sven fearlessly charge to her rescue!

© Disney

Blossoming romance

Kristoff and Anna are together at last. After all their amazing adventures, Anna finally realizes that Kristoff is the one who truly loves her.

© Disney

True love

Love comes in many forms—and it can catch you by surprise! Throughout their adventures, Elsa, Anna, and their friends come to realize that love is a force that is stronger than even the most powerful magic.

A father's love

When Elsa's magic grew stronger, the king was desperate to protect his beloved daughter. He tried everything he could think of to help her learn to control her powers.

A friend in need

Olaf lights a fire to help Anna keep warm, even though she tells him that the heat will cause him to melt. He explains that some people are worth melting for.

Brave heart

Anna sacrifices herself to save Elsa, just as her body turns to ice. However, Anna's act of true love thaws her own heart. The curse is lifted and she is saved!

Love will thaw

Anna's sacrifice helps Elsa understand her magic can be controlled by love, rather than fear. She finally knows how to lift the winter from Arendelle and bring back summer.

FROZEN II

Three years after Elsa and Anna reunited, things finally seem calm in Arendelle. But there are still so many unanswered questions. Where did Elsa's magic powers come from? What really happened to their parents? The sisters must go on an epic journey to find out the truth and discover who they really are.

Secret whispers

In Arendelle, Queen Elsa rules wisely, surrounded by her loving sister and loyal friends. But something unsettling is happening. Elsa keeps hearing a strange voice calling her to leave her kingdom and travel north. What could the voice mean?

© Disney

Elsa

Elsa cannot stop wondering where her magical powers come from. Nobody else in her family can create snow and ice!

© Disney

Anna

Elsa's sister, Anna, just wants her family—and Arendelle—to be safe. But life does not always turn out how you want it to.

Kristoff

Kristoff is devoted to Anna and he wants to marry her. Now he just has to find the perfect moment to propose.

Sven

Even with Anna in his life, Kristoff still relies on his trusted reindeer pal. Some friendships don't need words!

© Disney

© Dis

Olaf

Now that Olaf can read, he is learning all he can about the world. The little snowman's sense of wonder grows and grows with every book h...

© Disney

© Disney

Charades

The group always makes time for family game night. They have fun together, even when Elsa's clues are a little... tricky.

Story time

© Disney

As children, the princesses loved hearing the king and queen's tales of long ago. Their favorite was about an enchanted forest.

Sisterly bond

The sisters are very close. Anna can sense that something is bothering Elsa even before Elsa tells her about the voice.

To the north!

One night, the elements of nature suddenly leave Arendelle. Lights go out, water dries up, and a wind blows everyone out of their homes! Can the voice help Elsa undo this disaster? She follows it north to the Enchanted Forest. Inside, two old enemies—the Arendellians and the Northuldra—are trapped together.

© Disney

Ice crystals
Elsa's magic turns the moisture in the sky into ice crystals. As they crash down, Arendelle is thrown into chaos.

Not alone
To the north lies the vast Enchanted Forest that Elsa must enter. She is glad her friends are coming with her!

Explanation

The troll Grand Pabbie explains to Elsa that her powers have awoken the spirits of the forest, and they are still angry.

Mattias

Lieutenant Mattias has been trapped in the Enchanted Forest for over 30 years. He is fiercely loyal to Arendelle.

Magical mist

A strange mist blocks the way into the forest. When Elsa holds onto Anna's hand, the mist magically parts to let the group inside.

Ryder Nattura

Ryder Nattura is Northuldra. He dreams of being set free from the Enchanted Forest. He has never set foot outside it.

Honeymaren

Ryder Nattura's sister is bold and brave. She doesn't see Elsa and Anna as enemies, but as possible keys to freedom.

29

Courage calls

Everyone will need courage to complete their missions. Elsa must trust the voice and go where it leads her—alone. Anna must learn to let go of people she loves. And all of them must strive to free the forest and turn foes into friends.

Surrounded!
The Northuldra and the Arendellians are still at odds after all these years. They can't even decide who will take the group as their prisoners!

Familiar face
Anna recognizes Mattias from somewhere. She realizes that she has seen his face in a portrait hanging in the palace!

Floating off
Elsa is determined to face the dangerous Dark Sea alone. She creates an ice boat to send Anna and Olaf away from her and keep them safe.

Shipwreck
The voice leads Elsa and Anna to the wreck of an old ship. Its Arendellian flag identifies it as their parents' ship.

The Dark Sea

Elsa dives into the Dark Sea. Maybe the answers she seeks are on the other side—where her parents' ship was headed.

© Disney

Elsa's journey

Elsa's magical powers are hers alone. With great courage, she decides that she must finish her journey alone, too.

Elsa's message

Inside the cavern, Anna finds an icy message, sent from her sister across the Dark Sea. Suddenly, everything makes sense!

© Disney

Spirits of nature

The nature spirits are the most mysterious dwellers in the Enchanted Forest. These magical beings can be dangerous! They may help or harm, depending on how much respect they are shown.

Earth Giants

The Earth Giants are huge, craggy spirits who shake the ground with every step. They could easily crush a person.

Special scarf

Elsa and Anna have a treasured scarf that belonged to their mother. Honeymaren explains how the symbols on it depict the forest spirits.

Wind Spirit

The Wind Spirit can be playful or destructive. When it mixes with Elsa's powers it can stir up a magical breeze.

Fire Spirit

Fire breaks out whenever this salamander is upset. He needs to calm down again in order to put out his flickering flames.

Water Nokk

This powerful Water Spirit takes the form of a large, prancing horse. He can only be ridden by those he deems worthy.

Find stickers here for p2–3

Icy mountains

King
and Queen

Castle

Fjord

Duke

Lush
land

Close
sisters

Find stickers here for p4–5

Sisters in
the snow

Runaway

Stay
away

Living in fear

Finally
free

The
new queen

No way out

· ·

Find stickers here for p6–7

New beginning?

Lonely life

Knock,
knock

New friends

A brave journey

Anna's plea

Struck!

Find stickers here for p8–9

Full of hope

Important day

Keep control

Opening gates

Honored guests

Grand ceremony

Time
to dance

The truth comes out

Find stickers here for p10–11

Perfect
prince

Icy battle

Taking charge

Cold as ice

Power play

Exposed

Final fight

Becoming king

Opening up

Perfect pair

Shock announcement

Shall we dance?

True
love

Charmed

· ·

Find stickers here for p14–15

First
impressions

Mountain boy

Ultimate ice
sculpture

eindeer duet

Helpful plan

Sled upgrade

Troll friends

Find stickers here for p16–17

Heads up

Warm
introductions

Snowy playmate

Keeping cool

In summer

Warm-hearted reindeer

Speedy Sven

Furry friend

Tasty treats

Slipping

Beautiful patterns

Eternal winter

New look

Ice palace

Defense

Marshmallow

Fun on the ice

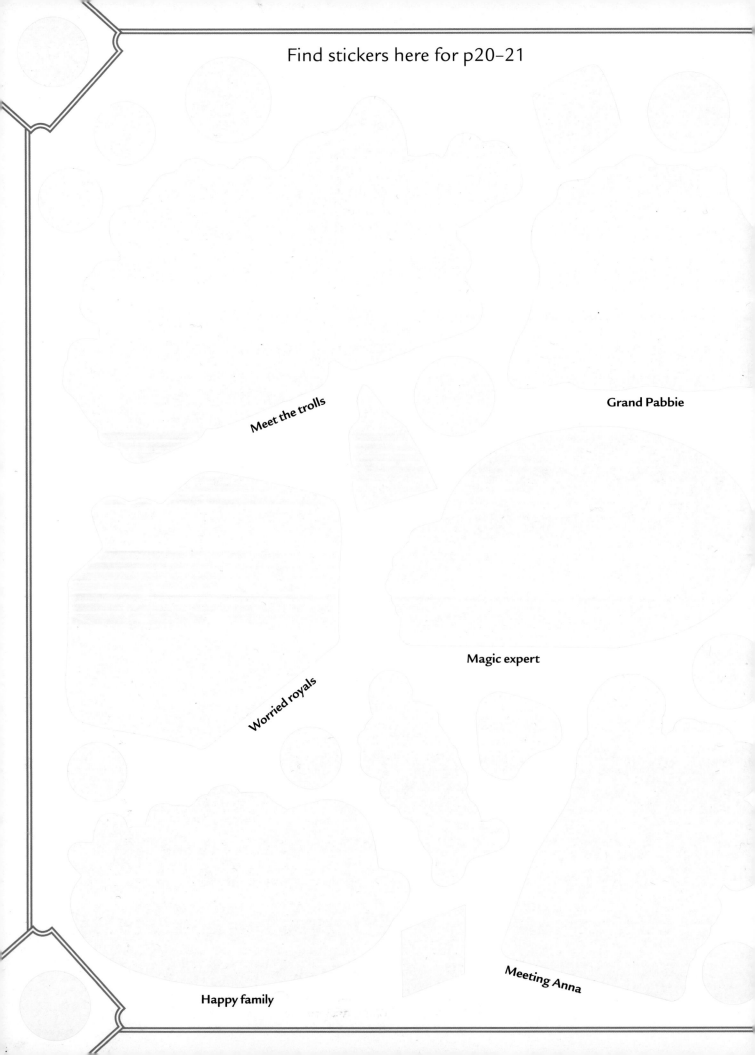

Meet the trolls

Grand Pabbie

Magic expert

Worried royals

Happy family

Meeting Anna

Frosty beginnings

Disagreements

A daring escape

Troll wedding

To the rescue

Blossoming romance

Find stickers here for p24-25

Brave heart

Love will thaw

A friend in need

A father's love

Find stickers here for p26-27

Story time

Sven

Elsa

Charades

Anna

Kristoff

Olaf

Find stickers here for p28–29

Magical mist

Mattias

Ryder

Ice crystals

Find more stickers here for p28–29

Explanation

Honeymaren

Find stickers here for p30–31

Surrounded!

Familiar face

Floating off

The Dark Sea

Elsa's journey

Shipwreck

Find stickers here for p32

Earth Giants

Water
Nokk

Special
scarf

Wind Spirit

Extra Stickers

Extra Stickers

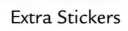

Extra Stickers

Extra Stickers

Extra Stickers